Millie

The Curious Mouse

Written and Illustrated by Paul Hyde

Paul Hyde

is a teacher, father, birder and wildlife enthusiast.

He has a degree in architecture and landscape and
a Masters in Education. He's from England but taught for 7 years
in Shanghai. He now lives in California with his wonderful
wife and beautiful daughter, Millie.

He was instilled with a love of reading from a young age
and now loves to doodle houses and wildlife, and to read
wonderful stories to his daughter.

Millie
The Curious Mouse

Written and Illustrated by Paul Hyde

To Millie and Catherine

Meet Millie. She's a mouse, the **PURPLEST** mouse around.

Even though she's tiny, her curiosity has no bounds.

She's always walking *round and round,* and up and down the street.

"Where's the fun, where are the games?" she'll ask, of anyone she meets.

Never far behind her, Mummy Mouse comes *racing* by,

"Have you seen my Millie, the one as purple as the sky?"

Meanwhile Millie h^{o}p$_s$ and s^{k}i^p$_s$ and discovers that birds can fly.

"Wow Egbert Owlie! How do you do that, so HIGH up in the sky?"

Egbert the Owlie said to find some higher ground,

She looks up and says, "Yes, the perfect place I've found!"

Millie climbs, scrambles and scuttles up towards the sky!
Egbert had said THIS is where you'll get to see them fly.

As soon as she's at the top, Millie looks near and far,

But Egbert said, "Wait, for a twinkle in the stars!"

By now Mummy Mouse had searched all over town,

And she was *very* tired of running up and down.

"Millieeeeee!!"

shouted Mummy Mouse as loud as she could.

Mummy Mouse found her at the top of the cliff.

"You scared me young mouse! You're my Millie Moo,"

"If something were to happen, whatever would I do?"

Mummy Mouse curled her tail around Millie, smiled and said...

"You're curious!"

"You're tough!"

"But flying like an owl? That's a little bit too much!"

I'm sorry Mummy, to give you a such fright,

But to learn more , Egbert said I need to see *them* at night!

"Them? Who is 'them'?" Mummy asked with a knowing smile upon her face.

"Look! The bats! They fly with so much grace!"

Mummy Mouse breathed out, smiled and then sighed.

As they watched the bats fly quickly,

swooping side to side.

"Isn't it amazing Mummy?"

"Yes my dear. But don't forget..."

Running.   Climbing.   Laughing.   Learning.

You are unique in so many different ways,

It's a joy watching you grOW each and every day.

Remember: you are my brightest star,

And no matter what you say or do, I'll still love you as you are!

I know Mummy Mouse,

and I love you too.

The end

Mummy and Millie Mouse set off for home.

Dinner was waiting...

How many did you find?

   ant

 ladybird

 bat

 owl

 glow-worm

 mountain goat

 squirrel

 spider

 rabbit

 earthworm

 grasshopper

Printed in Great Britain
by Amazon

87594405R00016